LEGO

NINJAGO
Masters of Spinjitzu

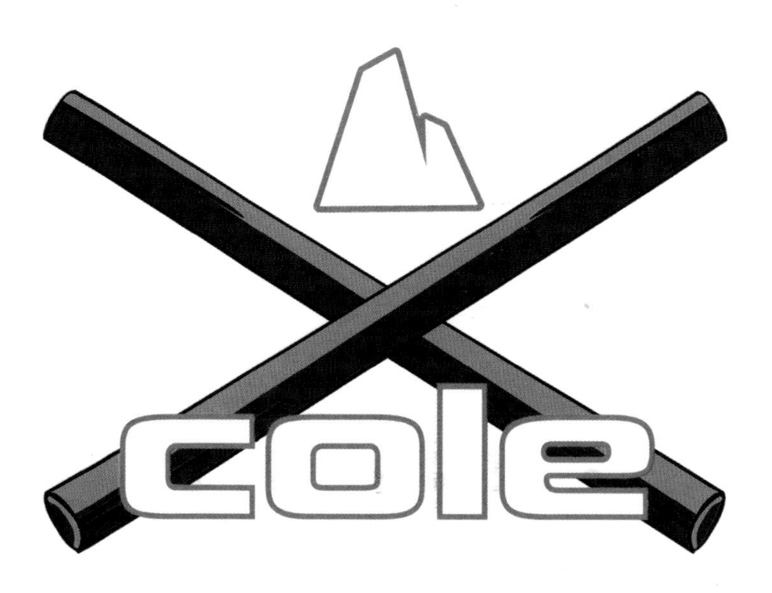
cole

Published by Ladybird Books Ltd 2011
A Penguin Company
Penguin Books Ltd, 80 Strand, London, WC2R 0RL, UK
Penguin Books Australia Ltd, Camberwell, Victoria, Australia
Penguin Group (NZ), 67 Apollo Drive, Rosedale, Auckland
0632, New Zealand (a division of Pearson New Zealand Ltd)

www.ladybird.com

"The Master of Earth", "The Real Hero",
"The Master of Lightning" and "The Dragon's Roar"
written by Greg Farshtey

Produced by AMEET Sp. z o.o.
under license from the LEGO Group.

Distributed by Penguin Books Ltd, 80 Strand, London, WC2R 0RL, UK
Please keep the Penguin Books Ltd address for future reference.

ISBN: 9781409310341
001 - 10 9 8 7 6 5 4 3 2 1
Printed in Poland

Contents

The Four Ninjas	4
Meet Cole	6
The Master of Earth	8
Ninja World: Stealth Warriors	14
Ninja World: Ninja Code	16
The Real Hero	18
Just Skulls and Dry Bones . . .	34
The Earth Dragon	36
Ninja World: Stealth Fashion	38
Ninja Quiz	40

The Four Ninjas

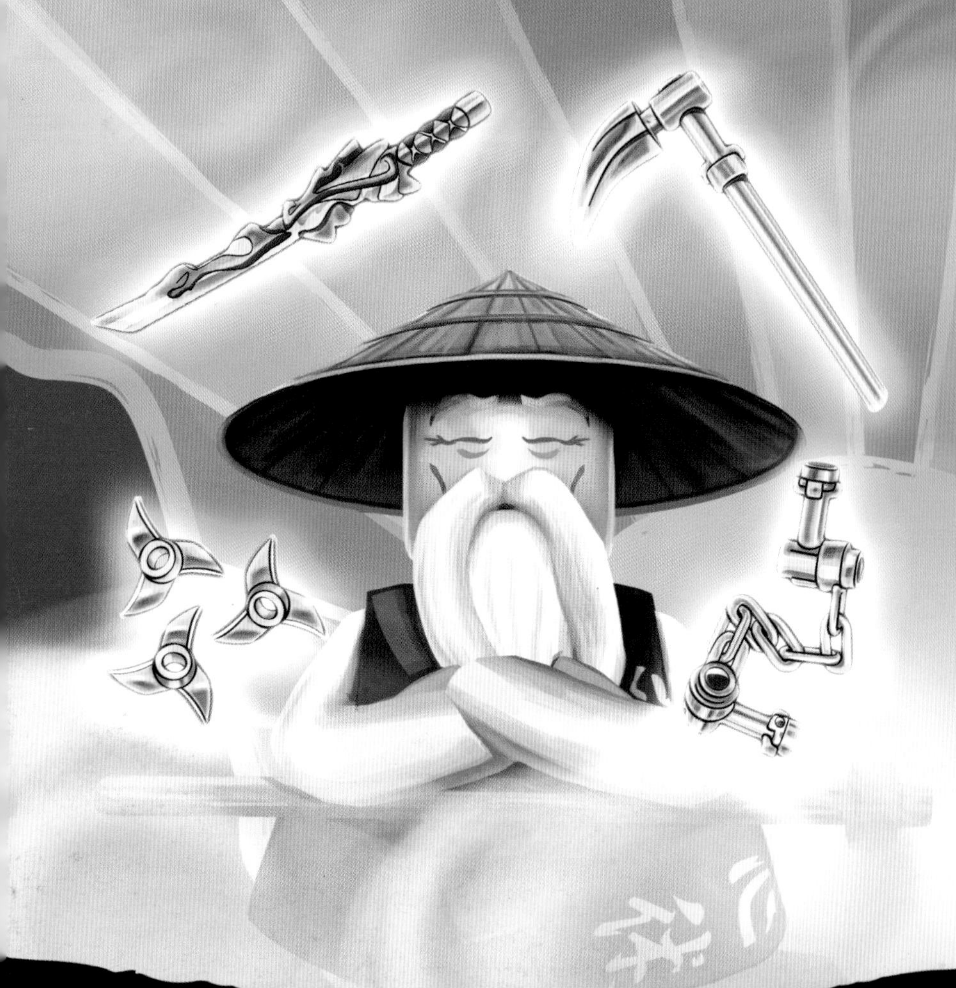

When Sensei Wu's evil brother, Lord Garmadon, threatened the peace of Ninjago, the Sensei went searching for four special boys – those who would have the ability to become ninjas. Garmadon wanted to steal the four powerful golden Weapons of Spinjitzu, and the Sensei needed the ninjas to help stop him. These four ninjas would need to harness an amazing power – the art of Spinjitzu – in order to fight Garmadon and his skeleton army. In this book, find out why the Sensei chose Cole and Jay, and learn how you too can learn the art of the ninjas...

Meet Cole

Personality:
Cole is the black ninja – a good friend and a strong, steadfast leader, although he can be a bit gruff

Element:
Earth

Skills:
Cole is very strategic and always makes the best plan for every situation

Weapon:
Cole used a bo staff – until he earned the golden Scythe of Quakes!

Cole is like an unstoppable force of nature – he always pushes himself to the limit. He would climb an impossibly high mountain and then tunnel through it just for pure pleasure! He is a skilled warrior who is afraid of nothing (except dragons – he's pretty scared of them). Cole is strong, reliable and as solid as a rock; he would never let you down and you would never find a better friend than him. The Sensei knew that Cole would make a great leader, and he was right – Cole's natural leadership skills showed as soon as he joined the team.

The Master of Earth

Cole is the leader of my ninja team. I did not assign him this job. To do so would have been to force him into a role he might not have been right for, and to force the others to become followers. I allowed the true natures of the four youths to shine through. It is Cole's nature to take charge in any situation.

It fits, therefore, that he is my Ninja of Earth. Like the ground beneath our feet, he is solid and steady. He puts the team first, preferring to focus on succeeding

in the mission than personal glory. He did not join my team out of a need for revenge, like Kai; or curiosity, like Zane; or a need for adventure, like Jay. No, Cole became a ninja because it was the right thing to do.

Well, perhaps that was not the only reason.

When I first met Cole, he was climbing a mountain most people thought could never be climbed. He was quite surprised to find me waiting for him at the top. As I talked with him, I learned that this was not the first time he had attempted something no one else could or would do. From sailing an unexplored ocean to skiing down an iceberg to hiking through trackless jungle, if it seemed impossible, Cole would try it. Yet, success brought no real satisfaction – it simply spurred him on to look for greater challenges.

Cole has many excellent qualities. He is strong, brave, smart, and disciplined. But he lacked purpose. He was like an axe honed razor-sharp, with no tree to fell. All the things he did to push himself to his limit served no other purpose than testing his endurance. Cole needed to know that all the things he could do, all his years of training, could in some way help others. I showed him that by learning to be a ninja and mastering Spinjitzu, he could be a part of saving this world.

How has he functioned as a leader? It has not been a simple task. His three partners are strong-willed, unique people, each of whom is part of the team for

his own reasons. Some, like Kai, have never been able to take orders from anyone. Add to that the urgency of our mission and there has been very little time for anyone to get used to functioning as a team, let alone having a leader.

Cole has handled this situation well. He never announced that he would be leading the team, for he knew that would provoke argument. Instead, he simply took command in the field as if it was the most natural thing in the world that he should do so. In the heat of battle, there was no time for the others to dispute his role. Once it became obvious that his first priorities were the mission and the safety of his friends, the others started to accept his authority.

Still, there is a darker side to all this. Cole takes his position very seriously and worries that he will let his team-mates down somehow. The night before a fight, Cole rarely sleeps, preferring to stay up and plan strategy. He trains constantly. The standards he holds himself to are far higher than those he measures others against. Cole will not tolerate any weakness, hesitation or failure on his part.

"These guys depend on me," he once told me. "If I freeze in battle, or I give the wrong order, or I haven't planned for every possibility, maybe someone gets hurt... or worse. That would put the mission in jeopardy, but more than that, it would mean a friend was harmed because I wasn't smart enough or quick enough. I won't let that happen."

And so, I watch Cole with some concern. He drives himself harder than anyone I have ever known and no man can do that for long. He will exhaust himself and that will not serve him or the team well. Even earth will crumble if too much pressure is applied.

For now, Cole will continue on. He will try to keep Kai from charging blindly into danger. He will encourage Jay to put his inventive skills to good use on behalf of the team. Zane may well remain a mystery to him, but Cole will try to make the Ninja of Ice feel part of the team. And just as they turn to Cole for guidance, I will try to remain someone he can go to for the same.

Ninja World: Stealth Warriors

Learn about the famous ancient shadow warriors with our fast ninja facts!

Ninjas were medieval Japanese warriors trained to carry out secret espionage missions. Like samurai, they were bound by their own strict code of conduct.

Ninjas practised the arts of stealth, fighting and survival. They were also amazingly skilled in engineering and chemistry: they made their own special weapons, explosive powders and even poisons.

Ninjas were organised into clans. Each clan would often have its own ryu – a unique philosophy and style of training and fighting techniques. The clans never revealed their secrets to one another.

The clan master was called the jonin. Middle rank ninjas – the clan elders – were called the chunin. They usually instructed the genin – the low-rank ninjas who actually performed ninja missions.

Ninjas were trained from childhood by their families. In early life toughness, agility and general athletic skills were emphasised. Later, fighting and specialised ninja skills were added to the training.

It was impossible to infiltrate a ninja clan – you were either born into it, or not in it. Being a ninja was a way of life, not just a profession.

The Sensei asks

If you managed to find the secret location of a ninja village, you would see dozens of black-clad warriors diligently training in silence. True or false?

Answer: False. A ninja village looked like any other medieval Japanese village.

Ninja World: Ninja Code

It may seem strange, but very strict principles can make one's life easier. Ninjas have their own set of rules, too . . .

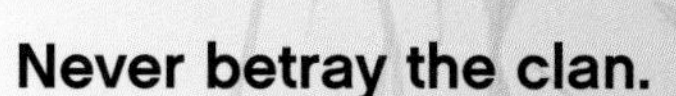

Never betray the clan.
Only if you are trustworthy and loyal to your teammates, will you succeed.

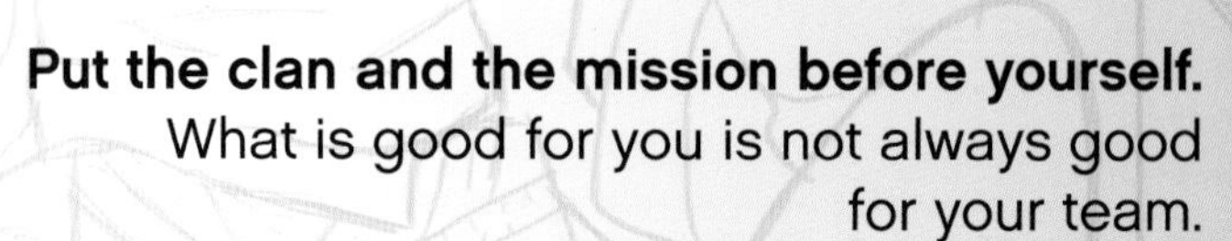

Put the clan and the mission before yourself.
What is good for you is not always good for your team.

Aid a genin from the same ryu.
Fellow ninjas need to support one another – loyalty and teamwork are true ninja values.

Constantly strive for perfection.
Your success and your survival depend on how good your skills are.

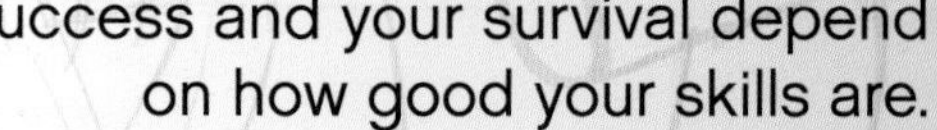

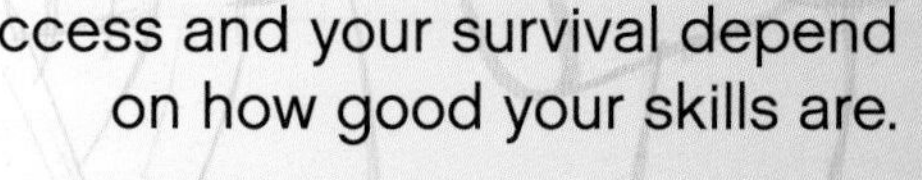

Never tell anyone you are a ninja.
Secrecy makes ninjas efficient. Your deeds should speak for themselves.

Always observe others and know your surroundings.
Better knowledge gives ninjas the advantage over their opponents in every situation.

Accomplish the mission.
When your actions are ineffective, withdraw, rethink your methods and start again! Failure is not an option.

Persevere in staying on your path.
No matter how hard it may be, don't give up – your goal is worth the effort.

The Sensei asks

The set of rules followed by the ninjas was called … hmm … What was it? I keep forgetting … Ninjato? Ninjago? Ninpo?

Answer: Ninpo.

The Real Hero

"Oh, you've got to be kidding me," said Jay.

"Why would we have done such a thing as a joke?" asked Zane, honestly confused by Jay's reaction.

"We're wasting time," snapped Kai. "Get out of the way and I'll go."

"No, I'll go," said Jay. "You'll charge in and get into who knows what trouble."

"Personally," said Zane, "I think I am the logical choice to . . ."

"We'll all go," said Cole, steel in his voice. "We're a team. Time we started acting like it."

The four ninjas stood on a high cliff overlooking a vast ocean. Dark clouds threatened overhead, bolts of lightning heralding the storm soon to come. The icy wind cut like a dagger and only Zane seemed not to feel a chill. That wasn't surprising, considering that one of Zane's hobbies was meditating at the bottom of half-frozen lakes.

The team had been successful so far, recovering two of the Four Weapons of Spinjitzu. Their quest had led them here in search of the Nunchucks of Lightning. But it wasn't the cliff, or the storm, or the cold that made them hesitate. It was the sight of an impossibly huge chain hanging in the air before their eyes. The links disappeared into the clouds far above.

There was only one way to find out where it led and that was to climb. Cole wasn't worried about that. He was an experienced climber, after all. What concerned him was his team: Kai, always so quick to rush into danger; Jay, constantly talking to cover his own fears; and Zane,

so cold and humourless he almost seemed like he was from another planet. Each was brave and skilled, but each also wanted to be the hero on every mission. It was Cole's job to keep them working together, but it was far from easy.

Cole glanced back at Sensei Wu. The Sensei nodded, once. Cole turned to his team and said, "Let's go."

Leading the way, Cole began to climb. He had learned long ago not to look down or to think about how far one might fall. Doing either one would keep a person from ever getting very high. Behind him, the others climbed in silence.

It felt like hours had passed before Cole's head broke through the clouds and the climb was at its end. If the chain itself had been a startling sight, what the Ninja of Earth now saw was even more amazing. Before his eyes were the ruins of an entire city – a floating city!

Cole pulled himself up and found his balance on an iron beam. The others quickly followed. “Wow,” said Jay. “I wonder what the rent was like on this place?”

“Fascinating,” said Zane. “I have never seen anything like it. Who built it? How does it float in air? Does anyone still live here?”

“Can we save the questions?” said Kai. “The only thing that matters is the Nunchucks of Lightning. In case you’ve forgotten, Samukai and his skeleton legion have my sister prisoner – and we know his warriors aren’t very far behind us.”

Kai took two quick steps along the beam. Suddenly, he lost his footing. Cole lunged and grabbed him before he could fall, hauling him roughly back to safety.

"No one has forgotten anything," said Cole sharply. "But you won't do your sister any good by getting yourself killed. Now let's search this place. The weapon must be here somewhere."

"It would be faster if we split up," suggested Zane.

Cole shook his head. "Too dangerous, Zane, we don't know anything about this place. Now, move out, but be careful."

The ninjas began to search. The city was incredibly ancient and looked as if it had been abandoned for many centuries. The design of the buildings looked like nothing anyone had ever seen before, but now the structures were covered in dust and shrouded in spider webs.

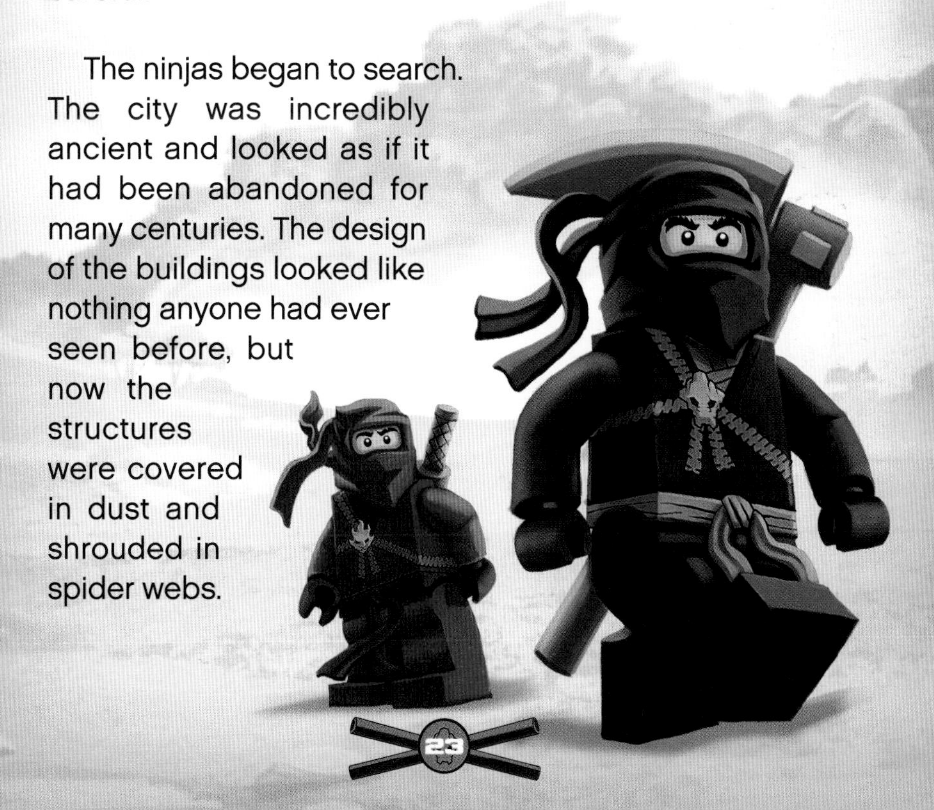

That would not have been so bad, except – as Jay discovered, to his regret – the spiders were four feet wide, had sixteen legs, and spat venom.

There were no obvious clues to who built the city, or to how or why they left. There was no sign of any current occupants, other than the spiders, some birds, and other wildlife. Here and there were scattered bits of rope, pieces of wood, fragments of cloth, and other debris. Some of the buildings were almost completely intact, while others looked as if they might fall down if anyone breathed too hard. All the while, lightning flashed overhead, as if the sky itself was angry at the trespassers in the city.

As the ninjas moved further into the heart of the city, Cole began noticing lightning symbols carved into the walls. At first, he thought they were just decoration. Then he realised that the bolts were pointing in various directions, almost like signposts.

"That's it!" Cole said. "The lightning carvings are pointing the way to the nunchucks. All we have to do is follow them."

"Let's hope that's all they're pointing towards," said Jay.

The ninjas moved swiftly through narrow, winding streets. At last, they reached a dead end. Before them was a vast building made of what appeared to be marble.

When Kai brushed against the stone, though, sparks flew, and so did he. As he got up off the ground, he exclaimed, "What was that?!"

"This is not any known type of building material," said Zane. "It's more like . . . solid lightning . . . but that makes no sense."

"If you expect things to make sense," chuckled Jay, "you're hanging around with the wrong people."

"We're going in," said Cole. "Be careful not to touch the walls . . . and let's hope the floors aren't electrified too."

Inside, the building was dark. Every now and then a lightning bolt from above would suddenly illuminate it, the light streaming through holes in the roof. The floor was made of earth and actually seemed to rise and fall beneath their feet. The interior walls crackled with electricity. All four ninjas could feel their hair standing on end from the energy in the air.

It was Cole who spotted the nunchucks. They were hanging from a metal hook high up on the south wall. It didn't take a genius to know that raw power was flowing from the wall through the hook, and that if anyone touched either, it might be the last thing they ever touched.

“I’ll get it,” said Jay. “I’m supposed to be Ninja of Lightning, so . . .”

“No,” said Cole. “Stay put. Zane, you know what to do.”

Zane nodded and took a shuriken out of his belt. He flung it at the east wall. It ricocheted off that to strike the north wall, then flashed to the west wall. Striking that, it shot for the south wall. The rotating blades sliced through the hook and both hook and nunchucks fell.

Jay took two steps, leaped, did a mid-air somersault and caught the weapon before it hit the ground. He landed on his feet with a smile on his face. “Got it!”

The earth floor suddenly heaved, knocking all four ninjas off balance. Considering that the team had already run into an Earth Dragon and an Ice Dragon on their quest, Cole had a bad feeling that he knew what was about to happen.

"Run!" he shouted.

As the ninjas fled the building, a Lightning Dragon erupted from beneath the earthen floor. With a roar, it charged towards the ninjas. Amazingly, it did no damage to the building. The solid stones of the structure turned ghostly, allowing the dragon to pass through as it pursued the heroes.

"The chain – head for the chain!" yelled Cole. Behind them, the dragon was breathing lightning bolts. One narrowly missed Cole, singeing his robe. "Kai, scout ahead, but keep it quiet!"

Kai moved with great stealth to the place where the ninjas had entered the city. He peered down the chain and saw armed skeleton warriors climbing up. Fortunately, they had not seen or heard him.

"We have company," he warned the other ninjas.

“Great,” said Jay. “Skeletons in front of us, Lightning Dragon behind – we’re going to end up as sandwich filling.”

Cole thought fast. “Maybe not,” he said. “We just have to learn to fly.”

* * *

Later, Kai, Jay and Zane would tell Sensei Wu of their adventure while Cole secured the nunchucks. It was the fastest job of inventing Jay had ever done. He lashed the pieces of wood together with the rope to form four frames shaped roughly like bird wings. Then he stretched the pieces of cloth across them to make crude hang-gliders. Using these, the four ninjas were able to escape the city with the nunchucks, soaring right past the enraged skeletons.

“So, you were the hero,” said the Sensei.

Jay shook his head. “No, not me... I mean, Zane was the one who threw the shuriken so we could get the weapon.”

“Then Zane was the hero,” said Sensei Wu.

“Well... Kai was the one who spotted the skeletons coming up the chain,” said Zane. “If not for him, we might have climbed down into a trap.”

Sensei Wu gave a slight smile. “I see. Kai was the hero, then.”

Jay frowned. "No, that's not right either. Maybe it was Cole? He suggested that Zane use his shuriken, and that Kai scout for us, and that I come up with a way for us to fly out of there. Is that being a hero? He didn't really do anything... did he?"

Sensei Wu looked at the ninjas. "Young ones, from what you have told me, Cole let the three of you use your skills to do what you do best, rather than trying to do everything himself. Sometimes, the real hero is the one who lets others be heroes."

Kai, Jay and Zane would think about that for a long time.

Just Skulls and Dry Bones ...

The army of the King of the Underworld is led by his three most trusted generals. All three of them have great strength and want nothing more than to destroy the living.

Nuckal is focused on fun... as long as 'fun' means smashing things up. His electrifying laughs are as dangerous as the axe he swings. Along with Kruncha, Nuckal wrecked Kai's workshop and accidentally found the map showing the hiding places of the Weapons of Spinjitzu.

Nuckal
First General of Samukai's army

Kruncha is as hard as a rock and about as smart as a rock, too. He is second in command to the King of the Underworld and he wants to take every opportunity to prove it... with his axe. His crazy attacks can flatten everything around him!

Kruncha
Second General of Samukai's army

Wyplash
Third General of Samukai's army

Wyplash always wants to know where he's been, so he often wears his head backwards. If he is not too busy wreaking havoc and mayhem in the world of mortals, he catches up on reading. The problem is, Wyplash likes to read the last page first... and that tends to ruin the story. Swinging his chains is a lot more enjoyable!

The Earth Dragon

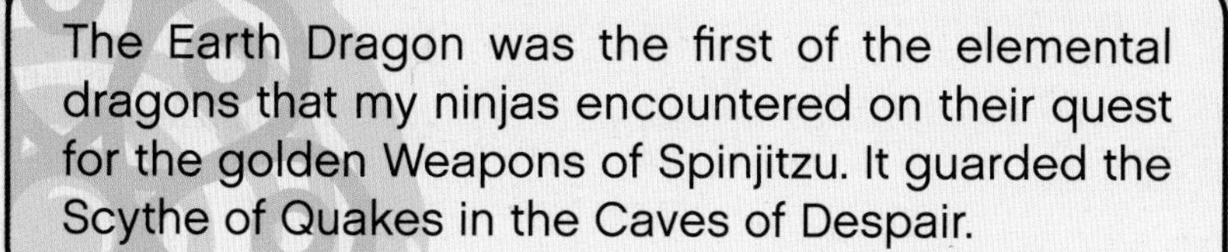

The Earth Dragon was the first of the elemental dragons that my ninjas encountered on their quest for the golden Weapons of Spinjitzu. It guarded the Scythe of Quakes in the Caves of Despair.

Rising from beneath the ground, the dragon scared away Samukai and his skeletons who were searching for the Scythe, but it did not manage to stop the ninjas who actually found the weapon and escaped with it.

The Earth Dragon did not hold a grudge against the ninjas for taking the Scythe. Some time later, it willingly answered the Fire Dragon's call to help the ninjas get to the Underworld.

Only the Ninja of Earth could ride the Earth Dragon . . . if the dragon would agree. Cole overcame his fear of dragons and simply commanded the dragon to give him a ride. The Earth Dragon obeyed.

Ninja World: Stealth Fashion

You've got to admit – ninjas look super-cool in their outfits! But the most important thing about ninja clothes is not their style, it's their functionality.

A Japanese martial-arts uniform is called "keikogi" or "dogi".

ELEMENTS OF THE NINJA OUTFIT

Shinobi shozoku

Black keikogi worn by ninjas. Various pockets and straps were hidden in the clothing to conceal weapons and ninja devices.

Sanjaku-tenugui

Headgear made from two three-foot scarves tied flexibly but securely around the head, leaving only the ninja's eyes uncovered.

Tabi

Ninja shoes – soft enough to be virtually silent. A split-toe design improved gripping and wall- or rope-climbing. Also known as "jika-tabi".

The Sensei asks

The Shinobi shozoku is traditionally black to make ninjas "invisible" in the dark. Black is always trendy, but do ninjas wear other colours as well?

Answer: Yes, for camouflage. White helps them to hide in the snow, dark green in the woods, and brown against bare earth.

Ninja Quiz

Can you rely on your memory, just like the ninjas and I can rely on Cole? Try this quiz, if you dare . . .

1. What was Cole doing when I first met him?
2. What is Cole afraid of?
3. Why did Cole endlessly hone his excellent skills?
4. What is Ninja Cole's element?
5. Why did Cole take command of the ninja team?
6. Who climbed up the giant chain to the floating city?
7. What led Cole to the Nunchucks of Lightning?
8. What made Cole a hero in his friends' eyes?
9. What colour clothes does Cole wear?
10. What is the Earth Master of Spinjitzu's weapon?

Answers: 1. He was climbing a mountain, 2. Dragons, 3. To be able to help others, 4. Earth, 5. Because he is a natural born leader, 6. All four ninjas, 7. Lightning carvings on the walls, 8. Ability to make the right decisions, 9. Black, 10. The Scythe of Quakes.

LEGO
NINJAGO
Masters of Spinjitzu

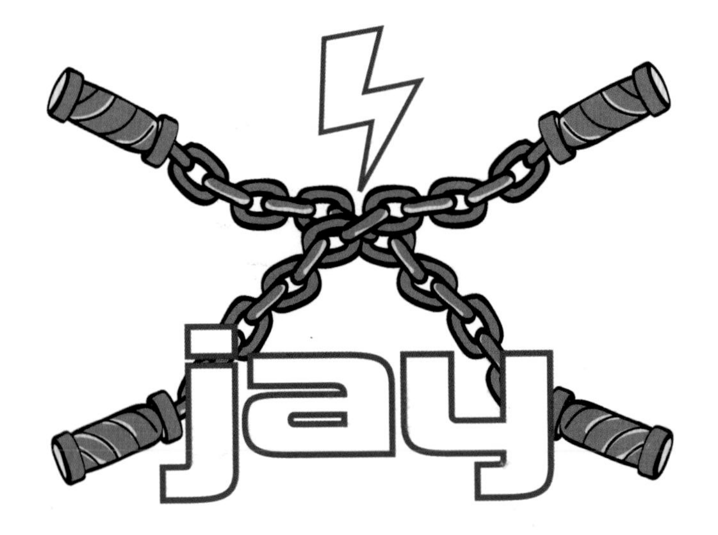
jay

Contents

Hope for Ninjago	4
Meet Jay	6
The Master of Lightning	8
Ninja World: Cool Inventions	14
Ninja World: Mythical Skills	16
The Way of the Ninjas: Core Principles	18
The Dragon's Roar	20
The King of the Underworld	34
The Lightning Dragon	36
Ninja Glossary Part 1	38
Ninja Quiz	40

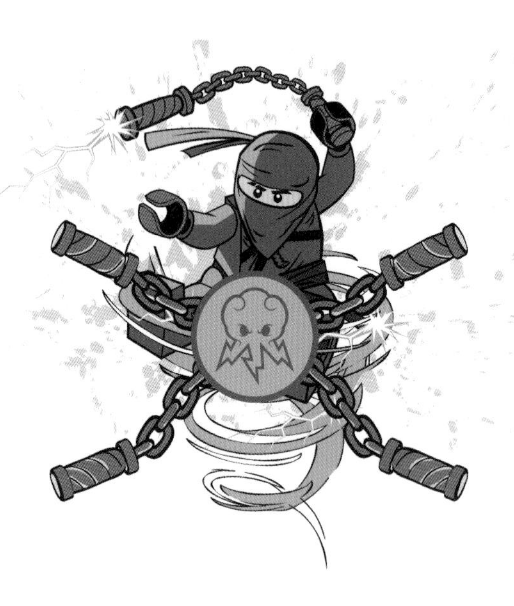

Hope for Ninjago

The world of Ninjago was in grave danger! Its future rested upon me and four young men: Kai, Jay, Cole and Zane. I did not choose them to join me because they were the world's greatest warriors – at the time they were not. But they each had a hidden power inside them. A power with which these four young ninjas could stop an entire army of evil skeletons...

5

Meet Jay

Personality:

Brave, creative and talkative, with a great sense of humour

Element:

Lightning

Skills:

Lightning-fast in combat, very good at inventing and . . . cooking

Weapon:

The Nunchucks of Lightning

With a heart for adventure, Jay has been in his element since he became a ninja. Sensei Wu's team jumps from one adventure to another, and Jay supports his friends with courage and amazing skills along the way. He loves tinkering with technology; he is smart and resourceful and solves problems with his crazy inventions. Jay loves telling jokes, too, but he saves them for his friends. His opponents get his fierce ninja flash-kicks and punches instead. Jay was the first of the four ninjas to discover the key to mastering the art of Spinjitzu. The Sensei couldn't have asked for a better Ninja of Lightning.

The Master of Lightning

A team needs many things in order to succeed. Unity, strength, skill, intelligence – all of these play a part. But one thing that is often overlooked is the ability to smile in the midst of danger. Heroes who can find humour in even the most perilous circumstances are often the ones best able to survive.

I know this well. In my time, I have encountered many adventurers who were grim and serious every moment. Few of them proved to be successful for very long. A hero has to venture into so many dark places and battle so many great evils that often only the ability to laugh at life can keep him going.

That is one of the reasons Jay is

such a valuable member of my team. He is always ready with a joke, even in the middle of a battle. His sense of humour sends a message to the others that everything will be all right, no matter what danger they may face together.

Jay is a young man of many talents. Along with being the Ninja of Lightning, he cooks, he builds models, and he has created many an invention. He loves to talk, leading Cole to refer to him as the "mouth of lightning." He seems to truly enjoy life and sees his career as a ninja as an excuse for endless adventure.

I first met Jay when he was testing out one of his inventions, a pair of wooden wings with which he was attempting to fly. Needless to say, it did not end well. I had already calculated the mass of his invention, the direction and speed of the wind, and the speed he would need to

successfully launch himself into the air. And so when his flight ended with him crashing into a billboard, I was waiting there for him.

Unlike Zane, who does not remember his past, Jay recalls it but does not wish to speak about it. I do not believe that he has some dark deed in his past that he is ashamed of, or anything of that nature. I think perhaps he came from humble beginnings and somehow believes that to be a cause for embarrassment. I cannot imagine why this would be so. A man, after all, is not measured by the wealth in his pocket, but by the riches in his heart.

Of course, there is now the matter of his obvious attraction to Kai's sister, Nya. He may well wish her to believe his

early life was an exciting one and the truth would be quite different. Still, if he truly cares for her, it would be best to be honest – for if she truly cares for him, she will accept him no matter how poor he might once have been.

Jay will tell you that he is a young man of many interests, but his true passion is inventing. He once told me that he has crates and crates of things he has created, some of which he can no longer recall the

purpose of or whether or not they work. Leave him alone for an hour with tools and raw materials and there is no telling what you may find when you return.

The list of his inventions is long and certainly unique. There is the machine that cores every apple on a tree, before they are even picked; the parchment that can be written on as a document, or stretched to form a waterproof tent; a blanket designed to keep a person cold on hot nights; and stilts that can telescope up and down, to allow someone to go from extremely tall to normal height at the touch of a button. (This last invention jammed on its first use, bouncing Jay between six feet and sixty feet high over one hundred times in two minutes. He said it took him a month to stop feeling dizzy.)

Still, all his creativity, humour and enthusiasm would mean nothing if he was not also a skilled and brave

fighter. Jay once took on an entire skeleton army in the Caves of Despair to buy his friends some time. He did not hesitate to do so, although it put his life in terrible danger. For him, there simply was no question – if Zane, Kai and Cole needed him, he would do whatever he had to in order to aid them.

Jay is truly a vital member of this team. I do not believe it could win without him, and I am not even certain it could exist without the qualities he possesses. Although he covers his feelings with jokes, I am sure he knows how proud his friends are to fight beside him.

Ninja World: Cool Inventions

The ninja's most powerful weapon is the mind. Knowledge of science combined with ingenuity enabled ninjas to invent many clever devices.

Torinoko

Small flash-bombs that exploded on impact, these caused a very bright flash that would temporarily blind anyone who looked at it. Ninjas used them mainly for distraction.

Shinobi Kumade

A 3-metre climbing pole with collapsible rungs and a large hook at one end. Each section could slide within another, to create a 1-metre length for easier transport and concealment.

Doka

A small container for safely carrying live coals. The device was useful for lighting fuses with minimum fuss. On a cold night, it could be used to warm fingers before a delicate task.

Mizugumo

A water-crossing device. The ninja wore these like shoes over his feet, balanced upright, and propelled himself with a paddle. Thus he could "walk on the water" – as long as the water was calm.

Tetsubishi

Small spiked metal devices, these were scattered on the ground and would pierce through the straw sandals of running opponents, slowing down their pursuit.

Metsubishi

A powder that temporarily blinded its victims, if thrown into their eyes or noses. Ninjas blew it at their opponents using a small box-like device with a mouthpiece at one end and a hole at the other.

The Sensei asks

Bored with their serious missions, ninjas often made fun of their opponents by secretly covering them with stink powder. True or false?

Answer: False. Stink powder was used as a tracking aid or as a ruse to get the opponent to remove his stinking armour.

Ninja World: Mythical Skills

People have always believed that ninjas were able to do the impossible. Did they really have supernatural powers or could they just use their abilities better than others?

Invisibility ...

... or disappearing in a puff of smoke were in fact smart tricks. Being experts in stealth and camouflage, ninjas were able to blend in with the environment or disguise their escape with smoke grenades.

Scaling vertical walls ...

... and jumping over incredibly tall fences are impossible for average people. But with their acrobatic skills, super agility and amazing tools, ninjas performed feats that were close to impossible.

Changing into other creatures ...

... or total control over animals are skills beyond human capability. Ninjas could at best train their pets, if they had any, and were unable to change their own human shape.

Making illusions . . .

. . . was just another skill that ninjas mastered to perfection through arduous training. Like today's circus magicians, ninjas learned many dexterous tricks to distract their opponents' attention.

Walking on water . . .

. . . or breathing underwater were thought of as superhuman abilities in ancient times. In fact, ninjas used a hollow cane as a snorkel and wore "water shoes" to walk on the surface of the water.

Casting spells . . .

. . . is a myth. Ninjas disregarded magic and relied on their clever technological devices, resourcefulness and finely honed skills at all times.

The Sensei asks

Bound by honour and honesty, ninjas officially denied having the superhuman abilities attributed to them in folk tales. True or false?

Answer: False. Some ninjas actually spread such stories themselves to increase their own value.

The Way of the Ninjas: Core Principles

Choosing the ninja path is easy. It is way more difficult to stay on it, though, for apprentice ninjas must accept a few principles . . .

1. Graduality

Start with simple assignments and slow exercises, and increase the difficulty and the speed of motions gradually. Ninjas avoid rushing into more difficult forms of training.

2. Continuity

Regular, systematic training with no prolonged breaks is the key to effective training. Ninjas practise every day with no exception, and keep to their training schedule.

3. Moderation

In order to achieve success in training, ninjas need to be moderate with earthly pleasures. Eating too much or spending too much time in front of the TV will diminish the effectiveness of training.

4. Self-Control and Self-Restraint

Train to stay calm and self-possessed at all times. Even under the most extreme conditions, ninjas cannot give way to their emotions – doubt, fear or aggressiveness.

5. Discipline and Courtesy

Behave in the most organised, disciplined and industrious way possible. Only such conduct shows the true respect an apprentice has for his teacher and for the art he is learning.

The Sensei asks

Does playing a ninja game on the computer for an hour a day give you almost the same practice as an hour of physical ninja training?

Answer: No. It is not even close to real training.

The Dragon's Roar

Jay was not a happy ninja.

In the last half-hour, the evil Samukai had succeeded in stealing three of the Four Weapons of Spinjitzu; Sensei Wu had vanished over a lava fall with the fourth; and Jay and his friends were unable to follow because Samukai and the Sensei were now both in the Underworld. Sensei Wu had counted on his new ninjas to protect the weapons from Samukai, and they had failed.

That was all bad enough. But then Kai suddenly appeared actually *riding* on a Fire Dragon. The great beasts, it seemed, were the key to following Sensei Wu. Being not truly of this world or any other, the dragons had the power to travel between Ninjago and the Underworld. First, though, the ninjas would have to master riding them.

Jay immediately sensed disaster. He saw only one slim chance of a way out. "Um, Kai, since yours is already taking passengers, why can't we all ride on it?"

Kai shook his head. "Each dragon will only carry a rider connected to its element – at least that's what the legends all say. So we each have to ride our own."

"I see two minor problems," said Zane. "First, we know nothing about riding dragons. Second, there are no dragons to ride."

"If that's what you see as 'minor' problems, I'd hate to see your idea of 'major' ones," said Jay.

"Whichever, we'd better find a way to solve them if we want to find the Sensei and get those weapons back from Samukai," said Cole. "We let ourselves be tricked like amateurs. Now we have to make things right."

Kai patted his dragon's scaly neck. "I think this big fellow here can provide one answer, can't you, boy?"

As if in answer, the dragon lifted its massive head and let out a long, low wail that seemed to last forever. This was followed by . . . nothing.

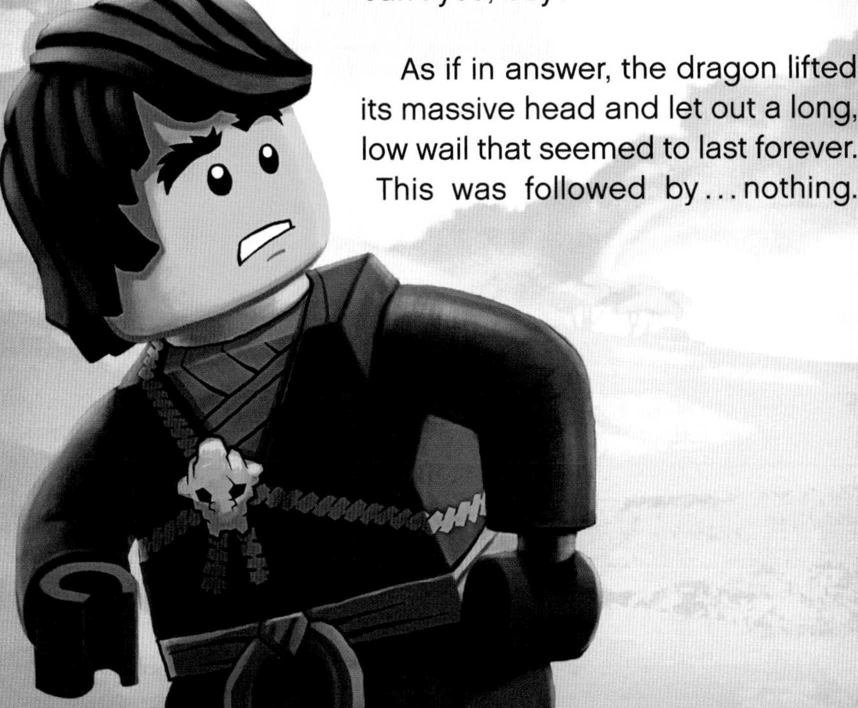

The ninjas stood around uncomfortably, not wanting to question Kai's judgment. Then they heard it – answering cries coming from the north, south, and west.

Cole pointed towards the sky. "Look! Look up there!"

High above, three great dragons were circling. The Ice Dragon was the first to land, followed by the Lightning Dragon and the Earth Dragon. They seemed to look at the Fire Dragon expectantly, as if to say, "Yes, what is it you wanted?" After a moment, they got restless and looked as though they were going to fly off. The Fire Dragon roared loudly and the other three immediately settled down.

"All right," said Kai. "Mount up."

"Wait just a second," said Jay. "How did you manage to get a dragon to let you ride it? I doubt it just let you climb aboard, unless it was looking for a potential snack on the go."

Kai shrugged. "Well, I guess I just explained to it what the problem was . . . and it wanted to help. If Garmadon is threatening the world, it's the dragons' world too, at least some of the time."

Jay had to admit that made sense, in a strange sort of way. Zane and Cole went right to work trying to persuade their dragons to work with them. Jay's dragon looked at the ninja through narrowed, serpentine eyes, as if daring him to try to be convincing.

"Right. Here goes," Jay said to himself. Meeting the dragon's gaze, he said, "Listen, there's this guy, Garmadon, and he wants to get his hands on some really powerful weapons – stuff that could even singe your scales. So you might want to, I don't know, help stop him."

At first, the dragon did not react at all. Then it took a long, lazy deep breath and exhaled, lightning bolts lancing from out of its mouth. "Yiii!" shouted Jay, barely avoiding being fried by dragon breath.

The dragon smiled and closed its eyes.

I should have known, thought Jay. *Each of us has a different talent, and Kai's is his energy and enthusiasm. He could probably talk Garmadon into giving up, if he had the chance. And Zane? He'll make a really logical argument to the dragon until it has to give in. Cole will just order the dragon to come along. But me? I'll have to do this a different way.*

Jay sat down on a hillside across from the sleeping dragon and thought about what he was good at. The first thing that came to mind was making jokes. Jay had a great sense of humour and always tried to keep his friends laughing. Maybe the dragon could use a laugh too. *If I smelled like that, I sure could*, thought Jay.

“Hey, dragon!” Jay said loudly. The dragon opened one eye. “How can you tell if you have a dragon in your bathroom? The door won’t close! How long was the dragon’s holiday? Four days and three knights! How about this one? Three ninjas and a dragon walk into a dojo, and . . .”

The Lightning Dragon swiped its massive tail, knocking Jay off his feet.

“That’s the worst thing about dragons,” muttered Jay, getting back to his feet. “They don’t know good jokes when they hear them.”

Jay went back to thinking. What else was he good at? Well, he was a pretty good cook. Even the Sensei seemed to like what he made over the campfire at night. Maybe he could make a tasty dish for the dragon.

Looking around, Jay was able to find many things for his recipe, including fruit, nuts, and various plants he knew were safe to eat. (Giving the dragon a poisonous plant for lunch would have been a very bad idea, after all.) He mixed them all together into a huge salad and used juice from the rillberry plant for a dressing. Then he placed the whole thing in front of the dragon's nose.

One eye half-opened and the dragon peered at his meal. It took a long sniff. When it breathed out, its electric power reduced the food to ash. Then it went back to sleep.

"I'll take that as a no," Jay grumbled.

"You made a salad for a dragon?" Kai asked, in disbelief.

"What's wrong with that?" said Jay. "Why, what do dragons eat?"

"Well . . . ninjas," said Kai, smiling, "especially ones who serve salads."

By this time, the young ninja was getting discouraged. Zane was already mounted on his dragon and Cole had his practically purring. Jay did not want to end up being left behind just because of an uncooperative dragon.

Think! he said to himself. *There must be something you haven't tried.*

Jay had one other talent, although not everyone called it that. He was an inventor, constantly tinkering with new gadgets and testing them out. Some of them didn't work and some of them weren't very useful, but he got a lot of satisfaction out of coming up with the ideas and putting them together. Maybe he could invent something the dragon would like.

But what would a dragon need, he wondered? It already had strength, the power of flight, natural armour, claws, and in this case, the ability to breathe lightning bolts. What would make its life better?

Then he remembered the Fire Dragon's roar. What if how loud the roar was determined which dragon was listened to? What if he could give the Lightning Dragon the loudest roar?

Jay hurried off to the cart and returned with an armful of tools and a bunch of odds and ends. He immediately set to work building a funnel-shaped device which, when spoken into, would make the sound much louder. That was nothing new, of course, but what made it unique was that it was designed to fit inside a dragon's mouth without interfering with the beast's ability to bite and chew. It was not perfect, he knew – after all, it was not as though he had the luxury of being able to measure the dragon's teeth. But if it worked, he could always modify it later.

When Jay was finished, he found he faced one more problem: getting the dragon to open its mouth long enough for him to put it in. The only thing he could think of was to make the dragon so angry that it opened up to breathe more lightning at him. And that was easy to do – he just made another salad.

This time, the smell of the rillberry dressing made the dragon more than a little irritated. It opened its vast jaws and prepared to add some sizzle to the recipe. As soon as Jay saw its mouth gaping wide, he rushed forward and put his invention into place. He was finished not a second too soon, as the angry dragon slammed its mouth shut and almost caught Jay.

"ROOOOAAAARRRR," said the dragon, so loudly that Jay was bowled over. The other dragons whipped their heads around in shock, and the mountains all around seemed to shake. The dragon roared a few more times, but with less fury and more a sense of celebration.

"So what do you think?" said Jay, back on his feet again. "Nobody's going to push you around again."

The dragon gave a low rumble of satisfaction that shook the ground beneath Jay's feet. Then it lowered its great head and allowed Jay to come close and climb atop its neck. Jay couldn't help grinning as he turned to his friends.

"What are we waiting for?" he said. "We have dragons to ride!"

The King of the Underworld

In the dark realm of the Underworld, a four-armed creature named Samukai ruled an army of skeletons. He hated the living so much that he made a pact with Lord Garmadon to destroy them. On my evil brother's order, Samukai's army raided the peaceful Ninjago in search of the four golden Weapons of Spinjitzu. The skeletons stole three of them from my ninjas and Samukai himself won the fourth one from me in a hard battle. With the powerful artefacts already in his hands, the King of the Underworld betrayed Garmadon and decided to keep them. Not for long, though, as a sudden burst of energy consumed him in a split second. Little did Samukai know that no one can handle the power of all the weapons at once...

The Lightning Dragon

I had hidden the Nunchucks of Lightning in a distant land where it seemed no one would ever want to seek anything. But if they did, they'd have to face the guardian of the weapon – the Lightning Dragon.

My ninjas found that desolate place and snatched the nunchucks. They swiftly flew away using Jay's smart invention – bat-like folded wings – narrowly escaping the angered dragon's bolts of lightning.

The Lightning Dragon met Jay again when the ninjas needed help with getting to the Underworld. At first, the dragon was not willing to cooperate, but Jay quickly gained its sympathy with a small roar amplifier.

The gift made the beast proud and happy. The Lightning Dragon not only gave Jay a ride to the realm where mortals cannot go, but also became his friend and accompanied him on many other adventures.

Ninja Glossary Part 1

In order to follow the way of the ninjas, you'll need to understand some special Japanese words . . .

aite – opponent

battojitsu – the art of using a sword in combat

bojitsu – a martial art employing a wooden staff

bokken – or "bokuto" – a wooden training sword

daimyo – powerful territorial rulers in medieval Japan who gave orders to ninjas

dojo – training hall in a martial arts school

genjutsu – the illusion techniques used by ninjas

kawanaga – a grappling hook with one to three prongs attached to a rope

ken – a sword

kunoichi – a female ninja

nawanukejitsu – a skill that allows ninjas to escape from bonds

ninja – or "shinobi" ("stealthy one" or "one who endures") – a person who studies and practices ninjitsu

ninjitsu – the ninja martial art covering mostly espionage and survival skills

saya – a sword scabbard

sensei – a teacher

shinobi aruki – the silent walk of the ninjas

shinobi-zue – sticks or staffs with weapons hidden within them

soke – a grand master

tanto – a knife

yari – a long Japanese spear

Ninja Quiz

Now, my young apprentice, it is time for a memory test. What do you remember of Jay's story?

1. What did Jay seek when he joined my ninja team?
2. What are Jay's talents, besides being a skilled ninja?
3. What device was Jay testing out when I first met him?
4. What kind of feeling has Jay got for Kai's sister, Nya?
5. Which dragon was to carry Jay to the Underworld?
6. What kind of food did Jay prepare for the dragon?
7. How many jokes did Jay tell the dragon?
8. What was the dragon's roar amplifier shaped like?
9. Which Weapon of Spinjitzu does Jay wield?
10. Which eyebrow on Jay's forehead is cut in two?

nswers: 1. Endless adventure, 2. Inventing nd cooking, 3. Wooden wings, 4. Attraction, . The Lightning Dragon, 6. Salad, 7. Two and half, 8. A funnel, 9. The Nunchucks of ightning, 10. His right one.